ECO ZICO

BY OLIVE O'BRIEN

ILLUSTRATED BY NINA FINN-KELCEY

Once upon a time, there was a little boy called Zico, who lived on the planet Zonar.

Everyone on the planet had a superpower, except for Zico.

Zico's father had eyes in the back of his head and could walk backwards without falling over.

His mother could see through walls. She often checked to see whether Zico was actually doing homework in his bedroom, instead of playing on the computer.

All the kids at Zico's school had amazing powers, too. One boy could fly and would swoop into the classroom with a swish of his cape. Another could make fireballs by clicking his fingers. One time, he had thrown a fireball at the teacher. She hadn't been very happy about it.

But Zico had yet to discover his superpower. It was so embarrassing.

The other kids at school made fun of him. "Zico has no superpower, Zico has no superpower," they chanted.

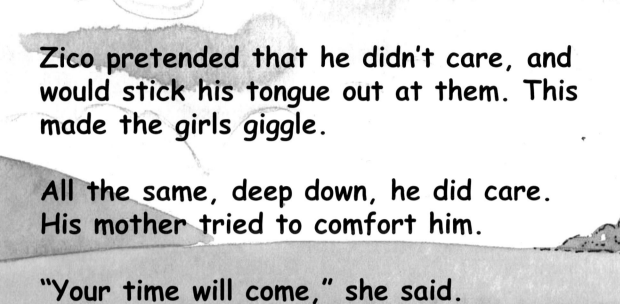

Zico pretended that he didn't care, and would stick his tongue out at them. This made the girls giggle.

All the same, deep down, he did care. His mother tried to comfort him.

"Your time will come," she said.

But Zico didn't want to wait. He hoped that he would discover his superpower soon.

"I wish that I could live somewhere like planet Earth. No-one has superpowers there and I would be like everyone else," he thought to himself.

So that night, while his parents snored loudly, he crept out to their space car. With a giant whoosh, it shot into the air.

Zico stared out the window as it hurtled past the stars, faster than the speed of light.

He couldn't stop smiling. No-one would laugh at him on planet Earth, he was sure of it.

But, the smile didn't last for long.

Through Zico's telescope, planet Earth had looked so blue and pretty. But, as the ship landed, he noticed that it was positively grey. The air reeked and made him cough.

Zico decided to explore the planet and went in the direction of a town called Greenville. But Greenville wasn't very green at all.

You see, the people who lived in Greenville were very lazy. They lay around all day snoozing and never bothered to clean up after themselves.

GREENVILLE

When they had finished their dinner, they threw mouldy cheese, rotting tomatoes and sticky bananas out the windows.

No-one ever bothered to reuse anything. "Recycling? What a waste of time!" they said.

So, over the years, gigantic mounds of rubbish had grown and grown, until they reached the sky.

Everyone in Greenville walked around with a clothes peg on their nose to block out the dreadful smell that wafted around the town.

The stench was so vile that Zico almost toppled over.

"Why do you have to live in such a stinky rubbish pile?" he asked the people of Greenville. "It's polluting your town."

"Why should we listen to you?" one man said.

"Well, Mister Litterbug, it will save you money, for one thing," Zico replied.

The townsfolk were intrigued.

"On Zonar, we stitch our clothes and make them as good as new, or take our shoes to the menders to make them last longer," Zico replied.

"I suppose we could all do with a little extra cash in our pockets," they said.

"And after my Mum makes me clean my room, I bring my old toys and books to the charity shop. Even if you don't want your old stuff, someone else will use it."

"This all sounds so boring!" one boy said.

"No way! It's great fun smashing and crashing glass bottles at the recycling centre. My Dad says that you can save energy if you recycle. We recycle many things and turn them into something useful again," Zico said with a smile. "If we all pitch in, we can tidy up this place in a flash," he added.

The townspeople all huddled together to decide what to do.

"I guess it would be nice to live somewhere clean for a change," they whispered.

"The flies that buzz around the trash are itchy and scratchy, and the rats' squealing drives me crazy," one girl admitted.

"Let's take a vote," the mayor said. "All in favour, raise your hand!"

With that, dozens of hands shot into the air.

The townsfolk took a leaf out of
Zico's book and transformed their
old junk into something marvellous.
They sorted the rubbish from the paper,
plastic, cans or anything that could be
recycled.

Soon enough there wasn't a speck of dirt to
be seen. The grey haze that had surrounded
the town lifted for the first time in years,
and the air was fresh and sweet-smelling.

The flies and rats didn't know what
to make of it all and stood there
with their mouths open. They were
astonished that the townsfolk had
cleaned up their act.

People from all over the world came to marvel at how clean and pretty the town was. They asked Zico to visit their towns too, to show them how he used his powers of persuasion.

The mayor of Greenville proudly declared it to be a green city. "You're a true superhero!" the mayor said. "Now, we'll have to call you Eco Zico."

GREENVILLE

The mayor gave him a smart cape with the initials "EZ" stitched in blue across it.

Zico smiled. He couldn't wait to return home to Zonar to tell everyone about his remarkable feat.

He didn't fly, or throw fireballs. He didn't see through walls, or have eyes in the back of his head. But, Zico did have the best superpower ever: the power to save a planet.

ECO ZICO'S TIPS FOR SAVING THE WORLD!

REDUCE!

Use less paper; when you do buy paper, make sure it is made from recycled materials.

Bring reusable bags when shopping, instead of buying plastic ones.

Use less of everything, including electricity. Turn off those light switches if you are not in the room.

Use less petrol. Petrol causes pollution. Walk, cycle or take the bus to school.

RE-USE!

Even if you don't want your old clothes or toys anymore, take them to a charity shop. Someone else will use them and the money will go to people who need it.

REPAIR!

Fix it and use it again.
Take your clothes and shoes to the menders.

RECYCLE!

Recycle your paper, plastic, glass bottles and aluminium cans. Turn them into something useful.

Recycling not only cuts down on waste. It also helps clean the air, water and earth.

Perry the Polar Bear is lonely and all he wants is someone to play with.

One day, he meets a baby seal called Sally, who is lost. The two set off on an amazing adventure to find Sally's family.

Will they succeed? Will Perry find a new friend in Sally?

ISBN 9780956384508

SILVER ANGEL

PUBLISHING